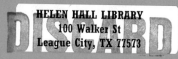

Groundwood Books / House of Anansi Press
groundwoodbooks.com

We acknowledge for their financial support of our publishing program the Canada Council for the Arts, the Ontario Arts Council and the Government of Canada.

 Canada Council   Conseil des Arts
for the Arts   du Canada

 ONTARIO ARTS COUNCIL
CONSEIL DES ARTS DE L'ONTARIO
an Ontario government agency
un organisme du gouvernement de l'Ontario

With the participation of the Government of Canada
Avec la participation du gouvernement du Canada | Canadä

Library and Archives Canada Cataloguing in Publication

Valério, Geraldo, author, illustrator
Blue rider / Geraldo Valério.

Issued in print and electronic formats.
ISBN 978-1-55498-981-2 (hardcover). – ISBN 978-1-55498-982-9 (PDF)

I. Title.

PS8643.A422B58 2018   jC813'.6   C2017-905230-6
C2017-905231-4

The illustrations were created with pen and color-pencil drawing, acrylic paint and collage.
Design by Michael Solomon
Printed and bound in Malaysia

FSC
www.fsc.org
MIX
Paper from
responsible sources
FSC® C012700

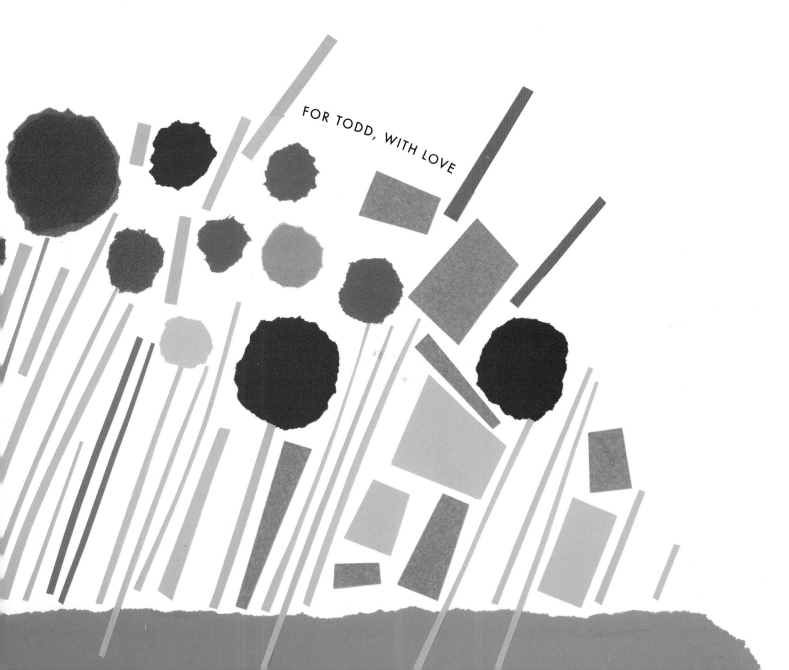

FOR TODD, WITH LOVE

BLUE RIDER

GERALDO VALÉRIO

GROUNDWOOD BOOKS
HOUSE OF ANANSI PRESS
TORONTO   BERKELEY

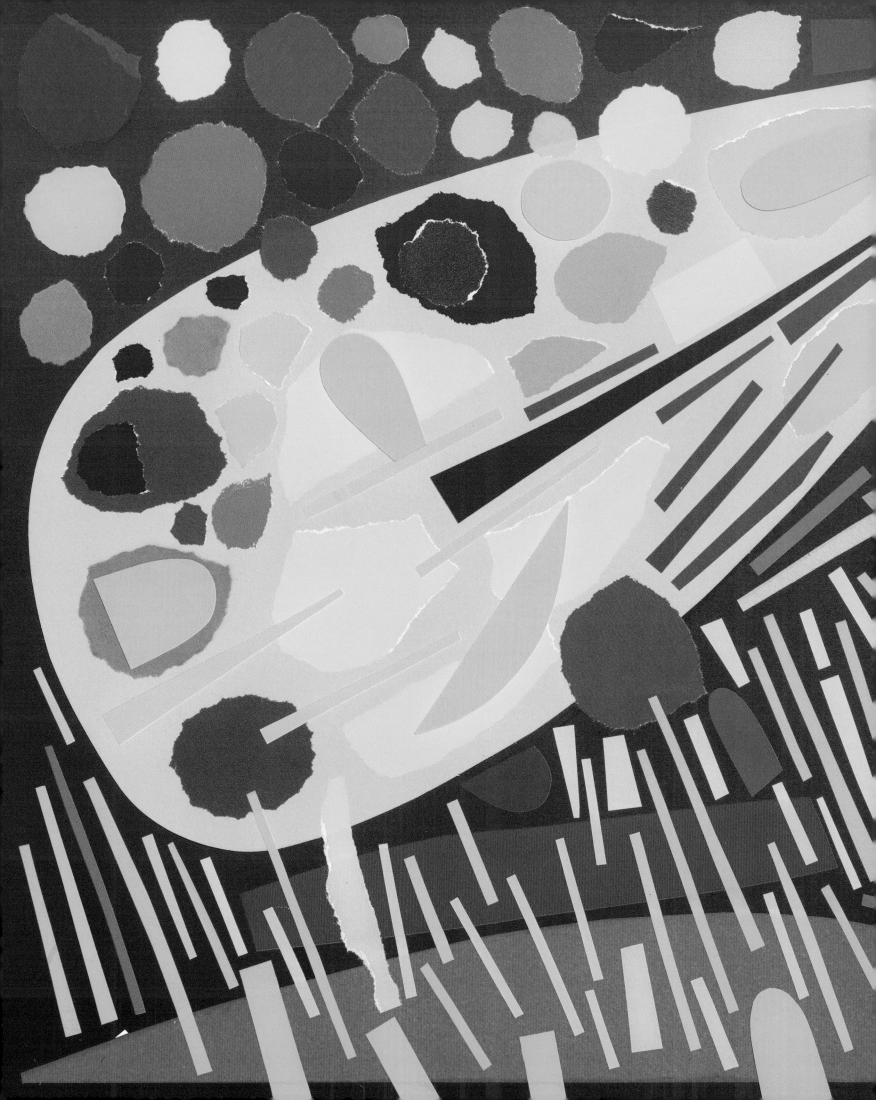